# Return to
# Ghost Camp

Look for more books in the Goosebumps Series 2000
by R.L. Stine:

# Return to Ghost Camp

AN
**APPLE**
PAPERBACK

SCHOLASTIC INC.
New York Toronto London Auckland
Sydney New Delhi Hong Kong

A PARACHUTE PRESS BOOK

ISBN-13: 978-0-590-68523-8

This edition is for sale in Indian subcontinent only.

First Scholastic printing, July 1999
Reprinted by Scholastic India Pvt. Ltd., September 2007
March 2008; January; August 2010; May 2011; January 2012
September; December 2013; September; December 2014

Printed at Magic International, Greater Noida

**I**'ll do anything you say. Just don't send me away."

"Dustin, there's nothing you can do to change our minds." Dad shook his head with disgust. "This is for your own good."

"If you send me away, something horrible will happen. I have a really bad feeling about this."

"You're not going to prison, Dustin. You're going to sleep-away camp." Dad sighed.

"Prison. Prison." Logan, my eight-year-old brother, jumped up and down on my bed, singing, "Dustin's going to prison."

"Shut up, Logan." I sat down on the floor and stared at the light-gray duffel bag at my feet.

DUSTIN MINIUM was neatly printed across the front in thick black Magic Marker. Mom made sure to use the kind of marker that doesn't wash off.

I looked at my clothes folded neatly on my bed. A stack of T-shirts. Jeans. Shorts. My mother was writing my name on everything I owned. Even my underwear.

"Dustin's going to prison." Logan jumped higher and higher.

"SHUT UP, Logan," I warned my brother.

Dad scooped up the stack of T-shirts and packed them into the duffel.

I glanced at my favorite Hulk Hogan poster hanging over my desk. Tonight would be the last night I'd see it for four whole weeks.

Four terrifying weeks at sleep-away camp.

How can they do this to me?

How can they send me away for four weeks?

I'll never survive, I thought.

I'm too shy to make new friends.

I'm too klutzy to play sports.

Maybe if I was built like Hulk Hogan, I'd want to go to camp, I thought. Strong arms. Muscular legs. That's what you need to be a good athlete.

But I'm not built like the Hulk. I'm really skinny. My arms and legs are perfectly straight. Not even a hint of a muscle. Even my straight brown hair looks skinny.

I'm a terrible athlete. A weakling. I can't squash a fly.

Flies.

Will the camp have a lot of flies? I wondered.

I hate bugs.

2

Sleep-away camp probably has lots of disgusting bugs, I thought.

Ticks that burrow under your skin and suck the blood right out of you.

Mosquitoes that make your brain explode when they bite you.

"Uh — do you think camp will have a lot of bugs?" I asked.

Mom and Dad rolled their eyes.

"Prison. Prison. Dustin's going to prison."

"SHUT UP, LOGAN!"

"Dustin's going to prison." Logan jumped so high he touched the ceiling. "And I'm going to take his room!"

"It's *my room!*" I shouted. "And you'd better stay out of it while I'm gone!"

"It's my room now." Logan pounded the mattress with his feet. *"Mine. Mine. Mine."*

I leaped up from the floor and tackled my brother in midjump.

"Stop, Dustin! Get away from me!" he yelled. "There's a spider on your arm!"

I jumped off the bed. Slapped at my arms. "Where? Where is it?" I cried.

"You're such a total wimp." Logan snorted. "I should be the one going to sleep-away camp. Not you."

Logan slid off the bed and started crawling into my duffel bag.

"Logan, get out of there." Mom dragged my

3

brother out of the bag. "You *are* going to sleep-away camp. Just be patient. You leave in a couple of weeks."

"But why can't I go now?" Logan whined.

"Because Dustin got the last place in the four-week program. We already explained this to you. You're going for the two-week program," Dad said. "Now, go to your room. Dustin's all packed, and he has to go to bed."

"I want to go to camp tomorrow," Logan complained as they left my room. "Why is Dustin always the lucky one?"

Lucky. Ha, I thought as I climbed into bed.

I pulled the blankets up to my chin. I settled my head deep into my pillow. And closed my eyes.

An hour later I was still wide awake.

Thinking about camp.

Thinking about no friends for a whole summer.

Thinking about bad food.

Thinking about mean counselors . . .

I must have fallen asleep right after that. Because the next thing I knew, I was standing outside my house, my trunk and duffel bag beside me, waiting for the camp bus to arrive.

It was a bright, sunny morning. The grass in our front yard sparkled with dew.

A big yellow bus roared as it turned our corner. I read the black letters painted on its side: CAMP FULL MOON.

4

Here is it, I thought miserably. Right on time.

The bus pulled up to the curb just as Mom, Dad, and Logan came out to hug me good-bye.

"I want to go," Logan griped as I dragged my duffel bag to the bus.

The bus doors opened.

I took a step inside.

Glanced up at the driver — and gasped.

His face was red and swollen — and covered with fleas.

Angry red blotches swelled on his forehead — raw, fresh flea bites, dripping with yellow gunk.

I raised my eyes to his hair — and screamed.

His hair was moving!

His hair was alive with fleas. Hundreds of fleas nesting in his scalp.

I watched them glide on their spindly legs. Glide along the bus driver's greasy brown hair. Glide until they reached the driver's cheeks. Then burrow under his skin.

I watched in horror as a flea leaped onto his nose. Started to gnaw at it. Dug in deeper, deeper — until a thin stream of blood trickled out.

Before I could move, the driver jumped from his seat.

He reached out for me with black-gloved hands. No. Not gloves.

His hands were black with fleas.

"Going to Camp Full Moon?" he snarled.

Then he reached out for me.

Grabbed my arms tightly with his flea-covered fingers.

"Let me go!" I screamed.

I twisted in his grip — and a swarm of fleas leaped from his fingers.

Landed on my arms.

Punctured my skin — and started to feed.

"L et go of me!" I cried.

I yanked my arms free from the bus driver's grip.

I swatted at the fleas. Brushed my arms frantically. But the tiny bugs dug deeper into my skin.

"Get them off me!" I shrieked. I shook my arms frantically. "Get them off! Get them off! Get them —"

Someone grabbed my shoulder. Shook it hard.

"It's okay, Dustin. You're okay."

I opened my eyes. My mother leaned over my bed, shaking my shoulder. Shaking me awake. "You were dreaming."

I sat up in bed. "It wasn't a dream," I croaked. "It was a nightmare. A horrible nightmare about the camp bus driver. He was covered with fleas."

Mom sat down on my bed. "Dustin, you have

7

nightmares about everything." She shook her head. "You have to lighten up. Stop being so timid about everything."

"I can't help it," I said. "It's just the way I am."

"Well, here's your chance to be different. You're going to a brand-new camp, with new kids you've never met. Try to be a different, braver person. If you think you're brave, you *will* be brave," she declared.

"Yeah. Sure," I muttered, still picturing all the fleas.

"A different person. A braver person," I mumbled to myself as the camp bus turned onto my block. "I'm going to be a different, braver person."

The bus pulled up to the curb. As the doors swung open, I remembered my nightmare. I held my breath — until I could get a look at the bus driver.

He was a young guy, wearing jeans and a navy-blue camp T-shirt with the words CAMP FULL MOON printed in yellow letters across the front.

I studied his face. No bugs.

I glanced up at his blond hair. No bugs.

I quickly checked out his hands. No bugs.

I let out my breath.

"Come on in!" He smiled. He loaded my duffel bag onto the bus, and we took off.

The bus was filled with kids. A few of them were

reading. But most of them were laughing. Joking around. A lot of them seemed to know each other already.

I took a seat by myself at the back of the bus.

I watched the other kids. Wondered if any of them would be in my bunk. Wondered if any of them would be my friends.

"We're making our last pickup," the bus driver announced. "Then it's on to Camp Full Moon!"

Everyone on the bus cheered.

The bus pulled to a stop. The doors opened and a kid about twelve, my age, got on. He wore khaki shorts, a black T-shirt, and black Nikes with no socks.

His brown hair stuck out of a black baseball cap, turned backwards. His face was covered with freckles — right up to his big green eyes. He was about my height. But he had muscles.

He sat down next to me.

"Hi. My name is Ari Davis," he said.

I told him my name and we started talking. He was a great guy. Really friendly. And a gymnast. That's why he had muscles. This was his first time at Camp Full Moon too.

"I can make a knock-knock joke out of any words," he said. "Try me."

"Okay," I said, thinking.

"Make it a hard one," he told me. "I'm really good at this."

I looked out the window as we drove by a firehouse. "Okay," I said. "Fire engine."

"Easy one," he smiled. "Knock-knock."

"Who's there?" I asked.

"Fire engine."

"Fire engine who?"

"Fire engine one and get ready to blast off!" Ari laughed. "Try another."

"Ari," I said. "Use your name."

He thought for a minute. Then he snapped his fingers. "Got it," he said. "Knock-knock."

"Who's there?" I asked.

"Ari."

"Ari who?"

"Ari there yet?"

His knock-knock jokes were kind of lame, but I laughed anyway. He had such a good time telling them.

"Do you like to play practical jokes?" He took off his baseball cap and tossed it on the storage rack above us.

"I've never really played one," I admitted.

"Never?" He raised his eyebrows in disbelief. "I play them all the time. I pulled off a really great one on the last day of school," he said.

"What was it?"

"I took the hinges off the art supply closet. When the teacher pulled on the doorknob, the door fell on top of him!"

I laughed. "Did you get into trouble?"

"Not for that one." He smiled. "But I got into trouble once for gluing my teacher's desk drawers shut."

I glanced out the window. The bus was leaving the city. We were on our way to Camp Full Moon.

I didn't have much time to worry about camp, though. Ari told me about a million practical jokes he had pulled. And before I knew it, two hours had passed.

"Hey! I've got a great idea," Ari said when we were almost there. "Let's play a practical joke on the counselors."

"Like what?" I asked.

"Let's switch identities. You be me. And I'll be you. Let's see how long we can fool everyone."

"I don't know if that's such a great idea. . . ." My voice trailed off.

"Come on! It'll be fun!" Ari gave my arm a friendly punch.

Wait a minute. Maybe it is a great idea, I thought.

Mom told me this was my chance to become a different, braver person. Maybe by pretending to be someone else, I could actually do it.

"Okay," I said. "Let's switch."

I gave Ari my backpack and he gave me his. We agreed to switch duffel bags too.

The driver drove up a grassy, tree-covered hill and stopped.

"Here we are," the bus driver announced. "Last stop. Camp Full Moon. Everybody off!"

Ari gave me his baseball cap as we left the bus. I put it on the same way he wore it, backwards.

"I'm Ari now," I reminded myself as I climbed down the steps. "I'm Ari."

But can I really be a whole new person?

# 3

"Nice cap, kid." A big man with a big, round belly gave me a slap on the back. He nearly knocked me to my knees. He spun my cap around — and nearly twisted off my head!

"Who is that?" I whispered to Ari when the big man had moved on.

"That's Uncle Lou," Ari whispered back. "I saw his picture in the camp brochure. He runs Camp Full Moon."

Uncle Lou looked older than my dad. He wore small wire-rimmed glasses that sat halfway down his long nose. He had a really bushy mustache and crazy eyebrows that grew straight out. Except for a fringe of black hair above his ears, he was practically bald.

He wore the same camp T-shirt as the bus

13

driver. But it looked much better on the driver. The T-shirt barely covered Uncle Lou's huge stomach.

He had on a pair of khaki shorts, brown sandals, and white socks pulled up to his knees. One of his socks had a hole in it. I could see his big toe sticking out.

In his hand he held a clipboard that he rested on his belly.

"Okay, listen up," Uncle Lou bellowed. "There's a place for everything. And everything in its place. Know what I mean?"

No one answered him.

"Full Mooners — stand over here." Uncle Lou pointed to his right. "New Mooners stand over here." Uncle Lou pointed to his left.

"What are we?" I whispered to Ari.

"We must be New Mooners," he guessed.

I gazed around the camp as everyone gathered into groups. A row of small cabins, all painted green, circled a sparkling blue lake. A diving board rose over one end of the lake. At the other end of the lake, a wooden dock and six canoes bobbed in the water.

Off to the side I saw a long cobblestone building. Probably the mess hall. And next to that stood a baseball diamond.

The camp was surrounded by thick woods. Archery targets hung on some of the trees.

"All Mooners, follow me!" Uncle Lou marched us toward the lake.

14

The ground was covered with a thick carpet of pine needles. It made the air smell sweet and piney.

Uncle Lou stopped at the row of cabins.

He called out names from his clipboard and started assigning bunks.

"I feel sorry for the losers who get that one." Ari pointed to a lone cabin that stood back in the woods. It was lopsided, with one end sinking into the ground. Most of the windows were broken. And some of the roof shingles were missing. A crooked sign over the door said CHEROKEE CABIN.

"Dustin Minium," Uncle Lou shouted out my name.

I was about to answer, but Ari cut me off. "Yo!" He raised his hand.

Uncle Lou checked his clipboard. "Cherokee cabin." He nodded toward the cabin in the woods.

Ari let out a groan.

"New Mooners always get the Cherokee cabin," a kid with bright red hair, freckles, and big hazel eyes leaned over and whispered. "It's the worst cabin in the whole camp."

Oh, great. I'll probably be in that cabin too, I thought.

"Maybe it's okay on the inside," I said, staring at the crooked building.

"The inside is nothing like the outside," the kid said. "It's *worse!*"

Ari groaned louder.

"Noah Ward," Uncle Lou called out.

"Apache cabin?" The red-haired kid shouted to Uncle Lou.

"Right-o, Noah."

"I knew I'd be in Apache," Noah said to me. "I've been coming here forever. I knew I'd get the best cabin!"

"Ari Davis," Uncle Lou called.

I raised my hand.

"Let's see." Uncle Lou peered over his glasses, skimming his clipboard. "Ah. Here you are. Apache cabin."

Huh?

"How did *you* get into the best cabin?" Ari groaned. "You're a New Mooner too."

"I-I don't know," I said.

Ari stared at the Apache cabin. It was the closest cabin to the mess hall. Its wooden shingles were coated with fresh green paint. White shutters covered the windows. It even had a porch.

This isn't fair, I thought. I should have been the one assigned to the Cherokee cabin.

But Ari didn't say anything about switching back. So I didn't, either.

"Hey, you're Ari Davis?" Noah slapped me a high five. "Wow! Okay!"

Noah turned to two guys standing next to him. "Ben! Jason! We've got Ari in our bunk!"

"Hey! We've got Ari!" Ben cheered. "All *right*!"

Ben was short and stocky and had curly brown hair.

"Yo! Ari!" Ben slapped me a high five.

"Ari — you the man!" Jason shoved Ben out of the way, which was easy for him.

Jason was built like a basketball player. He had really long arms and legs. His blond head towered over everyone.

Jason slapped me two high fives.

"Ari! Ari! Ari!" the three guys cheered.

What's up with these guys? I wondered.

I glanced at Ari. He didn't look happy.

Maybe I should end the joke, I thought. Maybe I should tell Uncle Lou about the switch Ari and I made.

"Uncle Lou?" I started over to him.

But before I knew what was happening, the three guys lifted me up on their shoulders.

"Ari! Ari! Ari!" they cheered louder.

What is going on? I wondered as they carried me off to our bunk.

Why are they so glad to see Ari?

"Hey, this place is pretty cool." The guys lowered me from their shoulders. I glanced around the cabin.

It had two bunk beds. Two small dressers. And a poster of Mark McGwire hanging on one wall. A dart board hung on another wall.

"Where is the counselor's bunk?" I asked.

"Apache cabin doesn't get a counselor," Noah said. "I told you — Apache cabin is the best!"

"I feel sorry for your friend Dustin." Jason shook his head. "The mosquitoes in that cabin will eat him alive."

"The mosquitoes aren't so bad," Noah disagreed. "The bedbugs are worse."

Mosquitoes? Bedbugs? Ari probably hates me by now, I thought. But this was his idea. Not mine, I told myself, trying not to feel guilty.

18

"Ari, give me your duffel. I'll help you unpack." Ben grabbed my duffel and started emptying it.

"You get the two top drawers," Noah said. "Only the best for you, Ari."

I watched in disbelief as he took my T-shirts and shorts from Ben and placed them neatly in the drawers.

What's *with* these guys? I wondered again. Are they this nice to everyone?

While Ben and Noah put my stuff away, I studied the bunks. The two top ones were really great. And one had a small window over it.

One of the bottom beds wasn't too bad, either But the other was in the darkest corner of the cabin.

That one will probably be mine, I thought. I'm the new kid here, so I'll get the worst bed.

I didn't mind, though. How could I — with everyone being so nice to me?

I sat down on the dark bed.

"Hey — you can't sleep there!" Jason protested.

"Sorry." I jumped up.

"That's your bed." Jason pointed to the top bunk with the window. The best one in the cabin.

"Are — are you sure?" I stammered.

"Sure, we're sure," Ben said. "You the man!"

Ben and Noah stopped unpacking and everyone gave me high fives again.

"Hey, Ari. Catch!"

I turned around and caught a candy bar Jason

19

tossed to me. As I unwrapped it, he guided me over to a big trunk.

"Look inside," he said.

I opened the lid and peered in. "Whoa!" The trunk was filled to the top with candy bars, soda, chips, and cookies.

"It's all for you." Jason grinned.

"Huh? For me?" I repeated, amazed.

"Yep." Jason plunged his hands deep into the trunk. He shoved fistfuls of candy at me. "You the man! Anything you want — just tell us."

"Anything," Ben repeated. "You just tell us."

"We can't believe how lucky we got. We can't believe you're in our cabin." Noah pumped a fist in the air.

"Why? What's going on, guys?" I asked.

The cabin fell silent.

The smiles faded from their faces.

No one moved. No one said a word. They stood there, staring at me strangely.

Jason lowered his eyes to the floor.

Ben folded his arms across his chest.

The room was so silent, I could hear my wristwatch ticking.

I shoved my hands into my pockets. I shifted my weight from one foot to the other, waiting for someone to say something.

Finally, Noah spoke. "You know why you're here, right?" he said quietly. "You know what you have to do? Right, Ari?"

I stared back at them.

My heart pounded in my chest.

"Uh . . . right," I said.

"Okay!" Ben unfolded his arms.

Jason tossed me a can of soda.

Everyone started unpacking their stuff. Telling jokes. Eating candy.

I climbed up on my bunk bed and watched them silently.

*What do they mean?* I wondered.

*What do I have to do?*

"So — where are we going?" I asked Noah that night.

"Just follow us," he said.

Noah, Ben, and Jason led me out of the cabin. I glanced at the cabins around the lake. At the trees edging the woods. All black shadows now.

"Let's go back to the cabin," I said. "I'll get my flashlight."

"We don't need a flashlight," Ben said. "We know where we're going."

"Um — where *are* we going?" I asked again, trying not to sound frightened.

"You'll see." Jason walked behind me. He gave me a shove from behind. "Keep walking."

We circled the lake. I heard the loud drone of insects. It was too dark to see them. But they seemed to be everywhere. Flitting in the tree branches above me. Nesting in the grass at my feet.

I heard croaking. Chirping. Buzzing.

I swatted a mosquito that buzzed in my ear.

*Where are they taking me?* My heart began to race.

Noah marched us across the front of the mess hall.

As we rounded the corner of the long cobblestone building, an orange glow lit up the night sky.

"Oh, a campfire." I let out a sigh of relief.

"It's a Camp Full Moon tradition," Ben said. "We always have a campfire the first night of camp."

The campfire blazed in the middle of a circle of stones. The whole camp was there — all the campers and all the counselors. Even Uncle Lou.

Kids stood around the fire. Or sat cross-legged in the grass. Eating hot dogs and chugging down fruit punch.

Off to the side, a long picnic table was piled high with a mountain of food.

"Sit right there." Noah pointed to a big boulder on the ground. "We'll get you something to eat."

I didn't want to sit by myself. I glanced around for Ari, but I couldn't find him in the crowd of campers.

"I'll go with you," I said. I jumped up and headed for the food table.

"No way," Jason declared. "We'll bring you plenty of stuff to eat. Relax."

The guys returned with hot dogs, juice, and fries. Before I finished my first hot dog, Noah jumped up and got me another one.

They stared at me as I ate.

"Everything okay?" Ben asked. "Do you need more mustard?"

"No, thanks," I said.

"Did I put *too much* mustard on your hot dog?" Noah jumped up again. "I'll wipe it off for you."

"Everything's great. Really," I said.

I bit into my second hot dog — and a giant bee landed on it.

I almost let out a shriek.

But the guys were staring at me.

I stifled my scream. I tried to slow my pounding heart.

I'm Ari now, I reminded myself. I'm a different person. I'm *not* afraid of bees.

I took a deep breath — then brushed the bee away.

But another bee began circling us. Then another.

Then dozens of them.

It was as if someone had upset a hive — and now the bees were upset with us!

They dove at the food. Circled the open juice bottles. Settled in the fries.

They buzzed around my head.

It was my worst nightmare.

I wanted to run.

I'm Ari now. I stared down at two bees buzzing around my hot dog. I'm not afraid of bees. I'm not afraid —

"ARI!" The real Ari called out to me. As he walked up to us, he scratched his arms. Then his legs. Then his arms again.

"Dustin! I've been looking for you!" I said. I dropped the hot dog and leaped to my feet.

"We'll be right back." Noah stood. "We're going to get you more juice."

"And marshmallows," Jason added. "I'll toast them for you. How do you like them? Black and crispy — or warm and gooey?

"Uh — crispy," I said.

"He's toasting your marshmallows?" Ari asked in disbelief. He pulled me aside. "Look, Dustin. I don't think this is working. I want to switch back." He scratched his cheek.

"Can't we do it just a little longer?"

He shook his head no. "This isn't fair. My cabin is the pits. There's a hole in the roof. The floor stinks from rot. And the mattresses are crawling with fleas." He scratched his head.

Ugh. Fleas. I took a step away from him.

"I know it's not fair. We'll switch back. In a few days. I'm having so much fun being you. Please," I begged. "Just a few more days."

"Give me a break," Ari said, bending down to scratch his ankles. "I think my fleas have fleas."

"Please. Just a few more days," I pleaded.

Ari let out a sigh. "Okay. But just a few more days."

He glanced over at the food table, where Noah, Ben, and Jason were piling my plate high with food.

"I should be the one getting the special treatment — not you," he complained.

"Why do they like you so much?" I glanced over at the guys.

Ari shrugged. "I don't have a clue."

"Hey, Dustin," one of Ari's bunk mates called out to him. "I'm ready."

"That's Melvin." Ari groaned. "I have to go. He wants to show me his shoelace collection."

Ari shuffled away, scratching the back of his neck.

I sat down on the ground, waiting for the guys to return.

I glanced at a kid I didn't know. He sat a few feet away from me, stuffing a handful of fries into his mouth.

Two bees landed on his plate.

He stared down at them.

A slow smile spread across his face.

Then, with one swift move, he scooped the bees up in the palm of his hand.

He lifted his hand to his ear. Listened to the trapped bees buzz wildly.

Then he brought his hand to his lips.

He popped the bees into his mouth — and swallowed.

id I really see that? I blinked hard. Did
that kid really swallow two bees?

I shook my head. No. He didn't swallow bees, I
told myself. Nobody swallows bees. It had to be a
hot dog. Two small chunks of hot dog.

"Yo! Mooners! Gather round!" Uncle Lou stood
in front of the campfire. "You know what they say:
Time waits for no one! So — let's get started."

Start what? I wondered.

I sat in front of the circle of stones and stared
into the fire. I watched the orange-and-yellow
flames lick the air. I listened to the sharp crackle of
the firewood as it burned.

I took a deep breath, breathing in the fire's
woody smell.

Maybe sleep-away camp isn't going to be so bad,
I thought. As long as I can be Ari.

"Okay! It's time for our traditional Full Moon welcome!" Uncle Lou announced.

He tugged his shorts up over his big belly. Then he lifted a whistle to his lips and gave a long, loud blow.

All the campers stood up. They threw back their heads and howled at the moon. Then they cheered: "Old Mooners. Full Mooners. Let's hear it for the NEW MOONERS!" Then they all howled again.

Ari sat down behind me. "This is a really friendly camp," he leaned forward and whispered in my ear. "I thought new campers were supposed to be treated like dirt."

"And a very special welcome for Ari Davis!" Uncle Lou pumped a fist in the air.

Huh?

"Ari. Ari. Ari," the whole camp chanted.

My cheeks grew hot.

"Ari. Ari. Ari," they cheered, stamping their feet, piercing the night with sharp howls.

"Apache cabin rules!" Noah shouted.

What is it with everyone around here? I wondered.

"They should be cheering for *me*." Ari leaned forward again. "This isn't fair," he whispered bitterly.

"We'll switch back soon," I promised.

A tall, skinny counselor carried a bench over to the fire. He had a buzz cut and a big space between his two front teeth. He set the bench down next to Uncle Lou.

"Nate, one of us has to lose sixty pounds," Uncle Lou joked. Then he lowered himself onto the bench.

"I think Uncle Lou is getting ready to tell us the story," Ben said.

The campers grew quiet.

"What story?" I asked.

But I didn't listen to the answer. I heard a rustling sound from the woods.

I turned and gazed into the dark trees that surrounded the campfire.

Something was out there.

I saw a pair of red glowing eyes. Animal eyes shining through the trees.

Then I saw a flash. Another pair of glowing eyes. Then another flash.

Dozens of red glowing eyes. Flickering in the woods. Staring at us.

A shiver ran down my spine as I watched the dark woods flicker with the eerie light.

What's out there? I wondered.

Whatever they are, I realized, they've got us completely surrounded!

"**T**his is the legend of The Snatcher,"
Uncle Lou began.

Everyone grew silent.

The campfire crackled behind Uncle Lou.

His voice was low. But I could hear him perfectly.

The campers sat totally still. Leaning forward slightly. Listening closely.

My eyes darted to the woods. To the glowing animal eyes flickering among the trees.

I wanted to ask one of the guys about them. Ask if they knew what was out there. But Noah, Ben, and Jason were leaning forward too, concentrating on Uncle Lou.

I turned away from the flashing red eyes.

I tried to forget that they were out there watching — staring at us.

31

"When the full moon rises — that's when he comes." Uncle Lou's voice grew lower.

"Who comes?" I whispered to Noah. "Did I miss something?"

"Shhhh." Noah placed his fingers to his lips. "Listen. Listen carefully, Ari."

"Come back with me." Uncle Lou closed his eyes. "Travel back twenty-five years — to a sunny day in July. Opening day of a brand-new camp.

"'A camp that should never have been built,' the local people said. They knew the danger. But no one would listen to them.

"Campers arrived all day long. They unpacked their bags and trunks. Laughing. Talking about the big campfire planned for that night. A big grand-opening celebration.

"And it was a big day for Johnny Grant. His first day at sleep-away camp.

"'Have fun!' Johnny's father ruffled his son's curly brown hair. 'See you in August!'

"Johnny's mother kissed him good-bye.

"She didn't know what was about to happen. How could she? Nobody knew."

"What didn't they know?" I heard Ari ask someone.

Someone shushed him.

"Finally the sun set," Uncle Lou continued. "It was a warm summer evening. A full moon hung in the sky. The lake seemed to glow under its soft, shimmering golden light."

As Uncle Lou spoke, I glanced over at the lake — and gasped. The lake was glowing! I gazed up into the sky — at the full moon that hung there.

This is just a story, I told myself. But I couldn't help it — I started to shiver.

"A campfire burned," Uncle Lou went on. "Campers gathered around it. Toasting marshmallows. So excited to be there. So excited to be the first campers at a brand-new camp — Camp Full Moon."

A soft murmur ran through our campsite. Uncle Lou waited for everyone to quiet down. Then he continued.

"After everyone ate and the fire died down, the counselors set out lanterns. The campers sat among the glowing lights. As they sang camp songs, a pack of red foxes gathered in the woods.

"They quietly made their way to the forest's edge. So quietly — no one heard them.

"They stared out from the trees. Stared out at the campers."

I thought about the flashing eyes in the woods. But I was too scared to see if they were still there. I kept my eyes on Uncle Lou.

Uncle Lou took a deep breath.

"Johnny Grant wandered away from the campfire. So happy to be at camp. So eager to explore. He headed for the trees.

"A few kids saw him leave. But no one called out to him. No one stopped him.

33

"Suddenly, a cry rang out from the trees. A voice screaming, 'Help me!' A tortured scream. A scream of pain.

"Everyone ran into the woods.

"They saw the foxes.

"But one of the foxes wasn't really a fox.

"It was The Snatcher.

"The local people knew all about The Snatcher. An evil creature that took the form of a fox. It hid among them and prowled the woods. Searching for its next victim.

"And now Johnny knew about The Snatcher too. His first day of camp — was his last. He was never seen again.

"Beware of The Snatcher," Uncle Lou whispered. "It can take any form. And it's watching. Always watching."

Uncle Lou opened his eyes. "Okay. Story's over."

I gazed around the campfire at the campers. At their terrified faces.

Why do they look *so* frightened?

I was scared too. But ghost stories are supposed to be scary. Aren't they?

"That was a good one," I heard one of the new campers say. "Uncle Lou tells great horror stories."

"The story is true," one of the counselors warned. "You'd better be careful. One kid van-

34

ıshes every year from this camp. Taken away by The Snatcher — and never seen again!"

"Yeah, right." The camper laughed. "Look at me. I'm shaking."

The campers slowly drifted away from the campfire.

Drifted back to their bunks.

I stared into the campfire. Watched the embers flicker and die.

When I started to turn away from the fire, someone grabbed me from behind.

I tried to scream — but a hand clamped down hard on my mouth.

I kicked and twisted — but I couldn't break free.

The hands gripped me tightly.

And dragged me roughly back into the woods.

**8**

"Let me go!" I struggled to cry out.

But the hand over my mouth pressed harder. Pressed my lips hard against my teeth.

I kicked. I twisted.

But I wasn't strong enough.

I was dragged deeper into the woods.

Out of sight of the glowing campfire.

"Okay. Let him go," a voice whispered.

The hands fell away.

I whirled around — and stared into Jason's eyes. Ben and Noah stood beside him.

"Sorry, Ari. Hope I didn't hurt you," Jason apologized.

I realized that my legs were trembling.

"Why did you drag me out here?" I shouted, trying to hide my fear.

"We want to talk to you," Noah said. "We have to make sure no one hears us." Noah's eyes darted from tree to tree.

"What's so important?" I asked.

He took a step toward me. "We have to talk to you about The Snatcher."

Huh?

"That dumb story?" I said.

"Why are you saying that?" Ben asked.

"Because that's what it is — just a dumb camp story," I replied.

"Oh, I get it." Jason smiled at me. "You're kidding around with us."

"Are you, Ari? Are you kidding around?" Ben demanded.

I didn't answer. I stared down at my feet. I kicked a rock in the dirt.

"You told us you understood." Noah stepped toward me. "In the cabin this afternoon — you told us you knew what you had to do." Noah's eyes narrowed. The muscles in his face tightened.

"Stop being so hard on him." Jason tried to calm Noah down. "Ari knows. Right?"

"Do you know?" Noah took another step toward me.

*What are they talking about?* My head began to throb. *What should I say?*

I backed away. Backed hard into a tree trunk.

The boys moved forward.

Started to close in on me.

*What do they want?* My heart began to pound.

I quickly glanced around.

The woods were dark.

We were totally alone out here.

They stepped closer.

*If I scream, will anyone hear me?*

"You the man, Ari," Ben said. "You're the one!"

They stepped closer — and I ran.

I darted through the trees, heading for the cabins.

I ran as fast as I could — searching for the clearing. Searching for the lake. Searching for the mess hall.

But I couldn't find any sign of camp.

I stopped. Spun around.

Nothing but trees.

*Where is the camp?*

*Did I get turned around?*

*Where should I run?*

The woods were filled with mosquitoes. They swarmed around my face. Flew into my eyes. Sunk their stingers into my neck, my cheeks.

I started to run again.

Mouth open. Panting hard.

Swatting mosquitoes.

I ran into a cloud of gnats. They flew into my mouth. My ears.

I shook my head wildly.

I ran and ran.

A sharp pain stabbed my side.

I stopped. Gulped air. Rubbed the pain in my ribs.

Heard the snap of a twig behind me — and froze.

I slowly turned around — and stared into the eyes of a fox.

A red fox.

Panting hungrily.

Staring back at me with glowing eyes.

I stumbled back.

    I kept my eyes on the fox.

*The Snatcher.*

The words floated into my mind.

Just a silly story, I told myself. Just a silly camp story.

Another pair of glowing eyes moved among the trees.

Then another.

All around me, the woods shimmered in red light.

The eerie light grew brighter as the foxes closed in.

My chest tightened.

I stared into a bright pair of eyes. Brighter than all the rest. Red-hot, intense as laser light.

*Are those the eyes of The Snatcher?*

Another pair of eyes loomed close by.

*Or are those?*

My heart raced. My clothes were drenched with sweat.

There were glowing red eyes everywhere I turned.

Just a story, I repeated. Just a story . . .

I spun away. Tried to run.

But I froze at the sound of an angry snarl.

And cried out in horror as a fox leaped into the air. Raised its paws.

Opened its jaws in an ugly howl.

And slashed its claws across my chest.

# 10

I heard a loud *RIP* as the sharp claws tore through my T-shirt.

"Help me!" I choked out.

The snarling fox fell back. Jumped up quickly. Prepared to attack again.

Behind him, I saw the other foxes, evil eyes glowing, move toward me. Heads lowered, they uttered low, menacing growls as they loped silently over the ground.

"Help!" I cried out. "Someone — help me!" But my shouts were smothered in the angry snarls.

The fox leaped again. Its claws raked my T-shirt.

The force of its body sent me sprawling onto my back.

The other foxes attacked. They jumped on me, snapping their jaws, clawing wildly.

I screamed again.

Twisted my body. Tried frantically to squirm away.

"Ari! Hold on!"

I recognized Noah's voice.

I saw him bursting through the trees, swinging a thick tree branch. He swung it at the foxes. Shouted at them. Kicked at them.

Still snarling, the foxes scurried into the woods.

When he was sure they were all gone, Noah dropped the branch and helped me up.

My legs trembled. I grabbed his arm to steady myself.

"Whoa. Are you okay?" he asked.

I checked myself out. My T-shirt was shredded. My shorts were ripped. I was covered in dirt.

"Ari, you shouldn't come out here alone. You're not ready to face The Snatcher — not yet." Noah shook his head.

I felt dizzy.

I didn't understand what he meant.

I leaned against a tree trunk. "Noah — what are you talking about?"

"You really don't know?" His eyes widened in surprise. "But we told you. You the man!" He grinned. "You're the one!"

"Stop saying that!" I demanded. "What do you mean? I don't know what you're talking about! Tell me NOW!"

"Okay. Okay." Noah stared at me. "If you really don't know, I'll tell you."

"I really don't know," I declared.

"You were chosen, Ari," he said. "You are The Snatcher's victim this year."

I stared at him. "You're joking, right?"

He didn't reply.

"Noah — this is just a joke you play on new campers — right?" I insisted.

He shook his head. He turned and began walking through the trees.

"Hey — wait!" I cried. I grabbed his shoulder. "Tell me the truth!" I demanded.

His eyes locked on mine. "I already told you the truth, Ari," he whispered. "The Snatcher is real. And you've been chosen. The Snatcher must have a victim every summer."

"But — but —" I sputtered.

"This year, it's you," Noah said softly. He turned and began walking again.

As we reached the edge of the woods, I could see the lake through the trees. The lake — glowing strangely under the full moon. Just as it did in Uncle Lou's story.

I thought about the foxes. The red foxes with the flickering eyes.

Uncle Lou's story had red foxes in it too.

Is the story true? I wondered. Is Ari the next victim?

*But I'm not Ari!*

Now I have no choice. I have to tell them the truth.

"Yo, guys. We're back," Noah pulled the cabin door open.

"Hey, man. You look horrible." Ben stared at my torn T-shirt and shorts.

Jason opened his stash of candy. He took a soda for himself and threw one to me.

My hand shook as I popped the lid. I took a big, long gulp.

"Listen, guys. I have to tell you something," I started.

They stood quietly, waiting for me to go on.

"I'm not Ari," I confessed.

I told them the whole story. About meeting Ari on the bus. About agreeing to switch identities.

"Ari thought it would be a great joke. So did I. But it's not funny anymore."

No one said a word.

They stared hard at me.

"Okay. You're Dustin," Noah said. "And I'm Uncle Lou!"

Noah grabbed Jason's pillow and stuffed it under his shirt. "See? It's me — Uncle Lou!"

Jason thought it was so funny, he spit his soda out.

"You know what they say," Noah bellowed, just like Uncle Lou. "If you spit straight up in the air, your head will get wet!"

Jason and Ben howled with laughter.

"Wait a minute. I just realized something." Ben turned to me. "You *can't* be Dustin."

"Why not?" I asked.

"Because I'm Dustin!" Ben started scratching his chest and legs. He slapped his arms, pretending to kill bugs. "See? *I'm* Dustin!"

"Give me a break!" I cried. "I'm serious!"

"Look, Ari." Noah wrapped his arm around my shoulder. "You have to be brave."

"But I'm *not* Ari!" I insisted. "You have to believe me. I'm Dustin. I'm telling you the truth!"

"Sorry. It won't work." Noah shook his head. "You won't get away from The Snatcher by pretending to be someone else."

I let out a sigh. I could see they weren't going to believe me.

We all climbed into bed.

Ben turned out the lights.

"Hey, Uncle Lou! Give me back my pillow!" Jason called to Noah.

The two guys fought over the pillow. Laughing. Having a great time.

47

I was still awake after the pillow fight stopped.
I was still awake after everyone had fallen asleep.

I'm going to find Ari in the morning, I decided.
And I'm going to tell him it's time to switch back.

Is that a terrible thing to do to Ari? I wondered.

But Ari *wants* to switch back, I decided. He
wants to live in the good cabin. He can't wait to be
Ari again. So I'm going to let him.

I closed my eyes.

But I didn't feel sleepy.

I sat straight up as I heard a scratching noise.

Soft at first. Then louder.

Animal scratches.

Animal scratches on the window screen.

Something was out there — clawing to get in.

Foxes?

*The Snatcher?*

I pulled the covers over my head.

Tomorrow I'll switch back with Ari. And everything will be okay, I told myself.

I didn't try to fall asleep.

I knew I wouldn't be able to — until I was
Dustin again.

# 12

"**O**kay, Ari. It's time to end the joke."

We sat in the mess hall, eating breakfast. Ari was stuffing pancakes in his mouth, two at a time.

I didn't feel like eating.

"Let's switch back," I insisted.

Ari glanced up from his plate. "No way. Take a hike. I'm Dustin."

"What are you talking about?" I cried in surprise. "You *said* you wanted to switch back. So okay. Let's do it."

Ari stuffed his last two pancakes in his mouth. Syrup dripped down his chin. "I'm Dustin. And I'm going to stay Dustin."

He picked up his plate. "Be right back. I'm going to get more."

What's up with him? I wondered. Panic made

my stomach churn. Yesterday he couldn't wait to switch back.

Ari returned with a plate piled high with pancakes. I stared at him as he ate.

"Oh, I get it!" I cried. "You heard — didn't you! You heard that you're supposed to be The Snatcher's next victim!"

"I don't know what you're talking about." Ari jumped up. "Come on. The senior campers are meeting at the boathouse. We're going to be late."

"Why? What's happening at the boathouse?" I asked.

"We're going kayaking. Remember?"

I didn't remember. I wasn't even sure what a kayak was, exactly.

Ari and I argued the whole way to the boathouse. No matter what I said. he refused to switch back.

"Two men to a boat! Heave ho!" Uncle Lou stood in front of the boathouse, bellowing orders.

Ben, Jason, and Noah were already there. So were most of the other senior campers. They carried the kayaks out of the boathouse and headed toward the woods.

"You guys are late." Uncle Lou shook his head. "Don't you know the early bird catches the worm?"

Ari and I lifted one of the long, narrow boats.

"Why are we going into the woods with these?" I asked.

"There's a river that cuts through the woods," Ari told me. "Don't you know anything?"

"I know who I am!" I dropped my end of the boat. "I'm Dustin. And I want to go back to being Dustin!"

"What's the problem here, guys?" Uncle Lou wandered over to us.

"I'm not Ari!" I blurted. "I'm Dustin. Ari and I switched names on the bus. Now he won't switch back!"

"Is this true?" Uncle Lou peered at Ari over his eyeglasses.

"No way," Ari said. "I can prove it."

Ari pulled a wallet out of his back pocket. "See? Here's my ID. It has my name and address on it. Dustin Minium, 2425 Westbrook Road."

Uncle Lou took the ID. "Yep. That's what it says."

"Of *course* it says that!" I shouted. "That's *my* wallet."

"Look." Ari pulled his T-shirt off. "Read the name on my shirt." He shoved the shirt at Uncle Lou.

"Dustin Minium," Uncle Lou read out loud.

"My mom wrote my name in everything." Ari smiled. "Want to see my underwear?" He started to drop his shorts.

"That won't be necessary, Dustin."

Uncle Lou pulled me aside. He placed his beefy

51

arm around my shoulders. "You've got to be brave, Ari. Don't try to put another boy in your place."

"I'm not!" I insisted. "You've got to believe me — I'm really not Ari!"

Uncle Lou took a deep breath. "You know what they say, son: When the going gets tough, the tough get going. Know what I mean?"

I shook my head. "No. I don't."

"It's simple." Uncle Lou narrowed his eyes at me. "Don't be a wimp."

I glanced over at Ari.

He and another kid were dueling with the boat paddles, laughing it up.

He's having a great time, I thought, and I'm going to be snatched away in his place.

It's not fair.

No one believes I'm *me*.

There must be something I can do.

But what?

e carried our boats down to the river.

The kayaks were two-man boats, with a cockpit for each guy to sit in, one behind the other.

I didn't want to ride with Ari, but the other guys had teamed up already. So I had no choice.

"Don't forget your skirt," Ari said to me.

"Huh?"

"Your spray skirt. You put it on, then attach it to the sides of the cockpit. It keeps the water out of the boat."

"Stop pretending to be nice," I told him.

"I'm not pretending." He smiled.

"Then switch back."

"Okay. I *am* pretending." He laughed.

Everyone climbed into the boats and we shoved off. No one seemed bothered by the millions of gnats that swarmed around us. So I tried not to complain.

I sat behind Ari. I'd never been in a kayak before. I wanted to watch the way he paddled.

I got the hang of it pretty quickly.

And I was starting to have fun.

The six Camp Full Moon boats skimmed along the water. It was kind of peaceful, gliding down the river. Slipping through the forest. Listening to the soft splashes our paddles made.

And then I heard another sound.

Voices.

From the woods on the other side of the river.

"Is there another camp over there?" I called to Nate, a counselor who manned the next boat.

"No," he stated firmly. "There are no other camps around here for miles. Keep paddling."

"Did you hear the voices?" I asked Ari.

"I thought I did," he answered.

We paddled some more — until we heard the scream.

A shrill, horrifying scream.

My heart skipped a beat as the scream rang through the forest.

"Who — who's in the woods?" I asked.

"It must be The Snatcher," Nate said. "Keep close together, guys."

Was he kidding?

I studied his face.

Waited for him to smile.

He didn't.

I tightened my grip on the paddle — and another scream rang out.

A shorter scream — cut off abruptly with a gurgling, choking sound.

I peered through the trees.

I saw something scurrying through the leaves.

What is that? I wondered.

I squinted harder.

"Oh, no," I moaned. "It's a fox."

"Knock-knock."

"Give me a break, Ari. I'm not in the mood for jokes."

We were carrying the kayak back to the boathouse. After we heard the second scream, Nate decided it was best to turn back to camp.

It was midafternoon now. The sun hung high in the sky. It was blazing hot. And I was sweating.

"Knock-knock."

"I said forget it."

"Knock-knock."

Why doesn't he just shut up?

"Knock-knock."

"If I answer you, will you shut up?"

Ari nodded eagerly.

"Who's there?" I mumbled.

"Dustin."

"Dustin who?"

"Dustin time to switch names!" Ari hooted.

"You're a riot." I let my end of the boat drop. I lifted my navy-blue Camp Full Moon T-shirt and wiped the sweat from my forehead. "Carry it yourself," I told him and stomped away.

Across the campground, I could see some kids playing baseball.

As I headed over to watch them, I saw a kid in the outfield catch the ball.

He threw it to the second baseman.

The second baseman missed the ball.

Whoa — wait!

The baseball flew right through him. It passed through his chest and flew out his back.

The pitcher caught the ball.

I squinted into the bright sunlight.

I'm seeing things, I told myself. It's the sun. It's playing tricks on my eyes. None of the players noticed anything strange.

The pitcher wound up and pitched.

The batter swung the bat. He swung too hard — and clobbered the catcher in the head.

You could hear the *THUNK* for miles! -

The catcher didn't fall.

He didn't cry out.

He signaled the pitcher for a fastball.

I stared hard at the catcher. At the second base-

57

man. A trickle of sweat dripped down my fore-head.

I'd better get out of the sun, I thought, heading for my bunk.

I'm seeing crazy things.

# 15

I sat in my bunk and listened to the kids diving off the diving board. Splashing into the lake.

It was free-swim time.

I told Uncle Lou I had to go back to the cabin.

"Okay, kid. But you know what they say: There's no sense in burying your head in the sand."

"Yeah, right." I had no idea what he was talking about.

"You never know what you can do till you try!" he called after me.

What *can* I do? I wondered, hunched on my bed. How am I going to get out of this mess?

Why didn't Mom and Dad listen to me? I told them not to send me here.

Wait a second.

I'll *make* them listen to me.

I'll call them — and tell them not to send Logan. I'll tell them to come pick me up. That I'm in danger here. Real danger.

I'll tell them to get me out of here right away.

Okay, I thought. Problem Number One solved.

That leaves Problem Number Two: Where is the phone?

"Yo!" Noah flung open the screen door. He was wearing his bathing suit, wet from swimming. As he crossed the cabin, he left puddles on the floor.

"I've been looking for you. How come you're not swimming?"

"Don't feel like it," I replied glumly.

"Do you *know* how to swim?" Noah studied me.

"Of course I know how to swim. Not great," I admitted. "But I know how."

I jumped down from my bunk. "Where's the phone around here?" I asked.

"It's right outside the mess hall. It's a pay phone hanging on the side of the building."

"Great!" I started to the door.

"No. Not great," Noah called after me. "Campers aren't allowed to use it."

That night, I waited for Noah, Ben, and Jason to go to the mess hall for dinner. I told them I'd catch up with them.

I peered out my window and watched all the campers making their way to the mess hall.

When I was sure that everyone was inside, I crept out of the cabin — determined to use the pay phone.

I approached the building quietly. Listened to the clattering of dishes. The clinking of glasses. The happy, laughing voices.

I tiptoed up to the mess hall window and stole a glance inside.

Yes. Dinner was under way.

I quickly made my way around to the side of the building — and gasped.

No pay phone.

Noah lied to me!

Why? I wondered. Why would he do that?

Oh. Wait. Maybe the phone is on the other side, I realized.

I walked around the back of the mess hall. I ducked beneath the windows so no one would see me.

I smelled hamburgers and french fries. My stomach rumbled with hunger.

But I couldn't eat.

I had to call home.

This phone call was going to save my life.

I turned the corner of the cobblestone building. Yes! There it was. The pay phone!

I dropped a bunch of change into the phone.

It fell down the slot with a noisy clang.

Did anyone hear?

I whirled around. No one in sight.

61

I dialed my number.

What if no one's home? I didn't think about that, I realized.

My stomach tightened as the phone rang.

*Please be home.*

Another ring.

*Someone, pick up the phone.*

Another ring.

"Hello?"

It was Mom. Yes!

I opened my mouth to speak — and a hand slid over my shoulder.

Reached the phone — and cut the connection.

# 16

I spun around to find Ari behind me. His eyes narrowed. "Who are you calling? You know it isn't allowed, *Ari*."

"And you know I'm not Ari!" I cried. "I'm calling my parents. I'm going to tell them to come and get me."

"Oh. Why didn't you say so? Let me help you." Ari grabbed the receiver from my hand. He gave it a strong yank — and ripped it off the cord.

"Here you go, buddy." He handed the receiver back to me. The wire dangled in the air. "Take it back to your cabin. Now you won't get caught."

"Why did you do that?" I shrieked. I threw the receiver to the ground.

"You can't go home." He slapped me on the back. "We need you, Ari. The camp needs you!"

"Stop calling me *Ari*!" I shoved him away.

63

"But you *are* Ari. You the man! Ha-ha-ha!"

"Laugh. That's okay. I'll be the one laughing on Monday. Because I've got bad news for you!" I told him.

"Yeah, what?"

"Knock-knock," I said.

"Give me a break." Ari shook his head. "What's the bad news?"

"Knock-knock."

"You're such a baby. You don't have any bad news."

"Knock-knock," I repeated.

Ari couldn't stand it anymore. "Who's there?" he growled.

"Logan."

"Logan who?"

"Wouldn't you like to know!" I said.

"You're a total geek," Ari said. "That's not a joke."

"Yes, it is." I said. "It's a joke. And the joke's on you. Monday!"

"Who's Logan?" Ari shoved me hard. I fell to the ground.

I grabbed his legs.

"Ooof." He fell on top of me.

"Give me back my shirt!" I clutched his T-shirt and pulled. "I want all my clothes back."

Ari climbed on top of me. He grabbed my arms and pinned them over my head. "What's the bad news. Tell me!"

I kicked my legs and sent him flying. He toppled into a tree.

"On Monday, my little brother is coming to camp," I told him.

I stood up and brushed the dirt off my jeans.

"And he'll tell everyone that I'm Dustin. Too bad. You lose."

"No way." Ari charged at me. He knocked me down again.

We rolled around in the dirt. Ari punched me in the stomach. I kicked him in the ankle.

"What's going on out here?" Uncle Lou came stomping out of the mess hall. He yelled for Nate to come outside.

Nate pulled Ari off me. Then he helped me up. "You'd better save your strength, Ari," he said to me. "You're going to need it."

"I'M NOT ARI!" I shouted. "I'M DUSTIN!"

"That joke's getting a little stale, kid," Uncle Lou said. "Why don't you just drop it?"

Ari laughed.

"Just wait," I said. "Wait till Monday. You'll see. You'll all see."

# 17

"**A**re you sure we're having a campfire tonight?" I glanced out the cabin window. "It looks like its going to rain."

"Then we'd better hurry," Noah said. He grabbed his sneakers and shoved his feet into them. "I have to win my bet."

"What bet?" I asked.

"Noah bet us he could stuff twenty marshmallows in his mouth at once," Jason said, pulling his Camp Full Moon T-shirt over his head.

"Yeah. And we bet him that we could stuff thirty!" Ben bragged.

"Want to bet with us?" Ben asked. "How many do you want to try?"

"Uh. I don't know," I murmured. "I never really tried to stuff my mouth with anything."

I opened the cabin door and gazed up at the sky.

Dark storm clouds drifted across the full moon. A strong gust of wind nearly blew the door shut.

I gazed at the rowboats on the lake. They pitched hard. Crashed into each other. Bobbed and reeled. Smacked against the wooden dock.

The campers were piling out of their cabins. With their heads down, they pushed against the wind, making their way to the campsite.

Ben shoved me out of the doorway. "Let's go! Before all the marshmallows are gone."

I followed the guys down to the campfire. A mob of kids already surrounded the food table.

Jason, Ben, and Noah elbowed their way through the crowd. Ben grabbed a fistful of marshmallows. He stuffed at least ten in his mouth before Jason and Noah started.

"Come on, Ari!" Noah shoved four marshmallows into his mouth. "Do it!"

"I don't think so," I said as Ben stuffed ten more in his mouth. His cheeks swelled up. "I'll watch."

"Look out!" Melvin, the nerdy kid from Ari's bunk, cried. "He's going to spew!"

Ben leaned into Melvin's face — and barfed out his marshmallows all over the poor kid.

"Here!" Jason shoved some marshmallows into my hand. "Your turn."

"Uh. Later," I said, backing away.

I turned and hurried toward the campfire.

I watched black curls of smoke rise from the flames, then disappear in the wind.

Tomorrow Logan will be here, I thought, staring into the flames. And I can go back to being Dustin.

"Still want to call Mommy and Daddy?" Ari stepped up beside me. "Hey, I've got an idea." Ari pointed to the fire. "Why don't you send them smoke signals?"

"Just wait," I told him, walking away. "Just wait until tomorrow."

I made my way around to the other side of the fire. I found a place to sit on the ground, behind a group of kids roasting marshmallows.

"Jeremy, do you have an extra stick?" a blond-haired kid asked his friend.

Jeremy didn't answer him. He was too busy shoving marshmallows onto his fingers. Wearing them like rings.

The blond-haired kid stared down at the marshmallow in his hand.

Shrugged his shoulders.

Then plunged his arm into the fire.

I shut my eyes tight.

*I didn't see that.*

I opened my eyes.

"Are you crazy?" Jeremy yelled at the blond-haired kid. "If you don't have a stick, do it this way!"

Jeremy stuck his fingers into the flames.

Everyone laughed.

*These kids are crazy!* I thought. They're going to burn their hands off!

I jumped up.

Another kid placed a marshmallow between his front teeth.

I watched in horror as he stuck his whole head into the fire. Flames crackled around him. The marshmallow between his teeth began to blacken.

Something is wrong here! I have to get away! I decided. I backed away from them.

This place is too weird. Too dangerous!

I took off, running for the woods.

I have to make a plan, I decided as I raced through the trees. I can't stay here. Not one more minute.

The wind blew hard through the trees.

The tree limbs swayed and creaked.

I heard the distant roll of thunder.

I pushed against the wind. Darted through the trees. Headed deeper into the woods.

The moon lit my way. But its light faded as the clouds rolled by it.

The wind gusted, blowing dirt up into my eyes.

I ran blindly through the trees. Tripping over tree roots. Scraping my arms against the rough bark.

Running with my head down. Running without looking.

"Hey! Watch where you're going!" a girl cried out as I plowed into her.

I gasped as she fell to the ground with a hard *THUD*.

69

She sat in the dirt, breathing hard.

The moonlight lit up the girl's face. She had blond hair, tied in a braid that hung down to her waist. Freckles dotted her small nose.

She wore blue cutoff jeans and a yellow T-shirt. A shiny silver chain dangled around her neck.

She gazed up at me with a frightened look on her face.

Who is she? I wondered as I stared into her deep-brown eyes.

Where did she come from?

held out my hand and helped the girl up. "Who are you? What are you doing out here in the middle of the woods?" I asked.

She brushed dirt off the back of her shorts. "I'm from the girls' camp."

Huh?

"What girls' camp?"

A clap of thunder boomed over our heads.

The girl didn't seem to hear my question. She gazed up at the sky and shivered.

"What girls' camp?" I asked again. "They told us there wasn't any other camp around here."

"They don't want you to know," she replied. "They're afraid boys will sneak over to our camp." She grabbed her braid and tugged on it tensely.

"Where is the camp anyway?" I squinted through the trees.

71

"You can't see it from here," she said. "It's on the shore of the river."

A few drops of rain started to fall.

"I'd better go." The girl turned to leave.

"Wait a minute," I said. "What's your name?"

"Laura Carter," she answered. "And you're Ari, right?"

A chill ran down my spine.

I stared into her dark-brown eyes.

"How — how did you know that?" I stammered.

# 19

"How do you know my name?" I demanded.

"I know a lot about you," she replied. "I know you hate bugs."

"How do you know *that*?" My voice shook.

"Don't get upset," she said. "I heard them teasing you."

"Who did you hear teasing me?"

"The other guys from your camp."

"When?" I demanded.

"When you were kayaking down the river. You didn't see me." She grabbed the silver chain around her neck and twirled it around her fingers. "I was spying on you through the trees."

The rain started to come down a little harder.

"I really should go," she said. "I don't want to get drenched. Then they'll know I was out here."

"*Who* will know?"

"The counselors at my camp," she said.

"Why *are* you out here?" I asked her. "Why are you alone in the woods at night?"

"Because I hate them."

Laura seemed nice. But she wasn't exactly easy to talk to. "*Who* do you hate?" I had to ask.

"Everyone and everything!" she muttered. "I hate all the other girls. I hate sleep-away camp. I hate it all."

She sighed. "I sneak away every night. And I walk in the woods. And I try to come up with a good way to escape."

She shrugged. "I haven't come up with a way yet."

"Aren't you afraid to be out here by yourself?" I asked. "Aren't you afraid of The Snatcher?"

Laura gasped.

"They tell you guys that story too? About a camper being snatched away every summer?"

I nodded.

"It's not true — is it?" Her whole body started to shake.

"I-I'm not sure," I stammered.

I felt awful. I didn't mean to scare her.

"I thought they made that story up," she said softly. "But if they tell you boys the same one — maybe it's true." Her lower lip trembled.

The leaves rustled behind us.

We both jumped.

74

I glanced behind me. Nothing there now.

"Just the rain on the leaves," I said.

"Okay." Her voice shook. "But we'd better head back."

"Look," I said. "I'm sorry if I scared you. I know how you feel. About camp, I mean. I hate it too. I'm totally unhappy there."

"You are?" Her eyes opened wide. "Great!"

"Great?"

"We can help each other escape!" Her face broke into an excited smile. "We can help each other get to the other side!"

"The other side of what?" I asked.

"The other side of the river. All we have to do is cross the river. And there's a highway nearby," she explained. "I was afraid to cross the river by myself. But now we can do it together!"

She grabbed my hand.

"Let's go!" She tugged me forward.

I can't go now, I thought. Logan is coming tomorrow. I can't leave him here by himself.

"Wait!" I pulled my hand free. "I can't do it tonight."

"Oh." Laura looked so disappointed.

"Let's meet tomorrow," I suggested. "We'll plan our escape."

"Do you promise?" Her voice filled with doubt.

"We'll meet right here," I said. "Do you think you can find this spot tomorrow?"

"No problem," she replied. "I'll just look for this

75

tree." She pointed to a tree trunk split down the middle. Then she said good-bye and hurried off toward her camp.

I headed down the trail. The rain started coming down hard.

I broke into a jog.

A bolt of lightning cut through the sky.

It lit up the woods for an instant.

But in that instant, I saw it.

A fox.

Standing at the end of the trail. Head lowered. Body arched.

Staring hard at me.

# 20

The fox trained its gaze on me.

I stood frozen. Barely breathing.

I stared into its eyes. Those eyes. There was something so human about them.

Something so familiar.

My heart pounded.

*I've seen those eyes before*, I decided.

The fox held me in its gaze.

What should I do? Should I try to make a run for it? Will the fox attack me the minute I move?

My heart pounded so hard, I thought my chest was going to explode.

I glanced down.

Saw a rock.

Picked it up in a trembling hand.

I took a deep breath. Gripped the rock tightly — then heaved it at the fox.

The creature jumped back, startled. It uttered an angry hiss.

Then scampered away.

I took off. I ran through the woods. Ran all the way back to camp.

The campfire was deserted now. The campgrounds were dark. The cabins were all dark too.

I had missed Lights Out.

I slipped quietly into the cabin and fell into bed. My heart still pounded.

Tomorrow is going to be a much better day, I told myself.

Tomorrow Logan will be here.

Tomorrow we'll both go home.

"What time is it?"

Sunlight filtered through the cabin window. I couldn't believe it was morning already.

I let out a loud yawn.

"Anybody know what time it is?" I sat up in bed.

The cabin was empty.

"Where is everyone?"

I jumped out of bed. And hurried to the window.

I saw some guys splashing in the lake.

Some of the younger kids were playing on the softball field.

What is everyone doing out so early? I wondered.

I found my watch on the dresser. Eleven o'clock! I slept right through breakfast. Through archery practice. Through tennis. How could it be eleven o'clock?

I pulled on a pair of black shorts and a black T-shirt. I jammed my feet into my sneakers and ran outside.

Uncle Lou walked out of his cabin, heading down the hill, away from the lake.

"Uncle Lou! Wait up!" I yelled.

I raced after him. "My brother, Logan, is coming today!" I told him, out of breath. "Do you know what time the bus will be here?"

"It's already here, kid. That's where I'm headed."

"Great! This is really great! Now I can prove to you who I really am!"

"Whatever you say, kid."

We headed down the hill together.

I saw the new campers empty out of the yellow camp bus. They stood in a crowd, waiting for Uncle Lou to greet them.

I spotted Ari, standing off to the side, watching us.

"There's my brother! The little kid in the orange T-shirt and the black baseball cap." I pointed out Logan to Uncle Lou.

"Nice hat, kid." Uncle Lou tugged on Logan's cap. "You know what they say: If you want to get ahead — get a hat."

"Uh. Thanks," Logan said.

"Logan! I'm so glad to see you!" I cried. "Tell

Uncle Lou who I am! Tell him I'm Dustin, your brother."

Logan stared at me.

"Who are you?" Logan murmured. "You're not my brother. There's my brother — over there."

He pointed to Ari.

"No, Logan — please!" I gasped.

But Logan ran over to Ari.

"How's it going, Dustin?" Logan slapped Ari a high five. "Who *is* that guy?" Logan asked, pointing to me.

# 21

"**L**ogan is *my* brother! You've got to believe me, Uncle Lou!" I pleaded. *"I'm Dustin!"*

I yelled so loud I could feel the veins in my neck popping out.

All the new campers stared at me in shocked silence.

Uncle Lou stared at me too.

Ari and Logan stared at me.

"He's crazy," I heard someone say.

"Calm down, kid." Uncle Lou took my shoulders in his big hands. "You're scaring the new campers."

I took a deep breath. But I couldn't calm down.

Ari headed toward the lake. I watched Logan walk off with him.

I shook my head. "I don't get it," I murmured. "Why is Logan doing this to me?"

"Listen to me, Ari —" Uncle Lou started.

"I'm *not* Ari!"

"Listen!" Uncle Lou said firmly. "It's settled. No more talk about who you are, okay?"

"I'm not Ari!" I insisted.

Uncle Lou sighed. "Okay. Look at it this way. I think you're Ari. Everyone in camp thinks you're Ari. Dustin's brother, Logan, thinks you're Ari. So give us all a break. Just *pretend* that you're Ari."

"*I'm* Dustin!" I shouted. "I know you think I'm crazy. But I'm not. I'M DUSTIN!"

Uncle Lou ignored me. He turned to the new campers. "Okay, listen up," he bellowed. "Full Mooners — stand over here...."

I wandered away in a daze.

Why did Logan do that to me? I wondered. I don't get it.

Feeling dizzy and frightened, I wandered down to the lake.

I watched some kids laughing and splashing in the water. They swam across the lake in a race. Then they all dunked underwater.

I waited for them to pop up again.

The water's surface turned smooth.

The air grew quiet.

No sounds of laughter.

No splashing.

How can they all stay underwater so long? I wondered. Where are they?

I started to worry. No one can stay underwater this long.

I stared hard at the lake.

*Where are you? Come back up!* I started to panic.

My heart pounded in my chest.

Something's wrong! This isn't normal!

"Help!" I screamed as loud as I could. "Somebody, help! They're all drowning!"

# 22

"They're drowning! Somebody — help!" I screamed.

My eyes darted around the campground, frantically searching for someone to help me.

The baseball field was deserted.

Uncle Lou and the new campers were nowhere in sight.

*Where is everyone?*

*Where are the counselors?*

"Help!" I cried out again. "They're drowning!" They'd been underwater for at least five minutes.

No hope.

No hope for any of them.

*SPLASH.*

The swimmers all bobbed up to the surface of the water at once. Laughing. Splashing each other.

How did they do that? I gaped at them. No one can stay underwater that long. *No one.*

There's something really wrong with this place, I told myself.

I'm getting out of here *today*, I decided.

But first I had to find Logan.

I didn't have to look far for him. He and Ari walked out of the woods. They headed for the canoes docked on the other side of the lake.

"Can we take a ride in one of them now?" Logan was asking as I walked up to them.

"Not allowed. We need a counselor with us," Ari told him. Then Ari spotted me. "Logan, listen to this great knock-knock joke."

"Logan doesn't want to hear your stupid jokes," I said.

Ari ingored me. "Knock-knock."

"Who's there?" Logan asked.

"Canoe."

"Canoe who?"

"Canoe believe how crazy he is?" Ari pointed to me.

Logan fell into a fit of laughter.

I let out a sigh. "Let's get out of here." I grabbed Logan's arm.

"Leave me alone." Logan yanked free. "You're not my brother. I don't even know you."

"Stop it, Logan!" I warned. "I said let's go."

I pulled Logan away. I found a place behind the mess hall to talk to him alone.

"What's going on?" I demanded. "Why did you say I wasn't your brother?"

Logan shrugged his shoulders.

"Answer me, Logan," I said through gritted teeth. "We're not moving from here until you tell me."

"Stop yelling at me." Logan pouted. "I'm scared."

Huh?

"What are you afraid of?"

"Ari. He said he'd hurt me if I didn't lie about you," Logan finally admitted.

I felt sorry for Logan.

"You don't have to be afraid anymore," I told him. "Tonight we're going to leave camp. We're going home!"

"I don't want to go home!" Logan jumped up. "I just got here. Why do we have to leave?"

"Because it's dangerous here."

"No, it's not. I just have to pretend you're not my brother."

I didn't want to tell Logan about The Snatcher. Or all the weird things I'd seen the kids doing around here. He was already scared. I didn't want to make things worse for him.

"Go to your bunk and unpack," I told him. "Everything will be okay. I'll see you later."

I sat by myself for a while and came up with a new plan. A pretty good one, too.

I'll meet Laura in the woods later, I decided. I won't take Logan with me. I'll go by myself.

Laura and I will escape to the highway on the other side of the river. We'll find a phone.

Then I'll call Mom and Dad and make them rescue me and Logan.

Now that I had the plan worked out, I felt a little better.

I decided to go to my cabin and wait until it was time to meet Laura.

I ran along the path that led to my bunk.

I saw a few kids up ahead holding bows and arrows. I recognized a couple of them from the mess hall. One kid was tall and skinny with black hair. His name was Todd.

Todd slipped the arrow into his bow.

He took aim.

I followed his glance — and gasped.

He was aiming at another camper. A short, chubby kid named Billy.

Billy stood with his arms outstretched — and he already had an arrow sticking out of his chest!

Billy was the target!

Todd pulled his arm back — and let the arrow fly. It flew straight into Billy's shoulder.

Billy didn't cry out. He didn't even flinch. Grinning, he started to pluck it out.

"Leave it there!" Todd called. "I want to see if I can shoot another one right underneath it."

I started to cry out — but Todd let another arrow fly fast.

He missed. It didn't hit Billy's shoulder. It flew right into Billy's forehead.

"Stop it!" I yelled. "You're *sick*!"

Todd and the other kids turned to me.

Giggling, they aimed their bows and arrows at me.

I turned and ran.

I charged into the woods to hide. To wait for nightfall. To wait to meet Laura.

I sat down on the ground and leaned up against a tree.

Will I find a way out of here? I wondered. Will I really escape this terrifying camp?

I peered up into the dark sky.

The light of the full moon peeked through the leafy treetops.

It's time, I thought.

I took off through the forest to meet Laura.

The steady drone of crickets filled the woods. Their chirping seemed to follow me wherever I turned.

I ran until I reached a fork in the path.

Which way? Left or right?

I searched for something that looked familiar. But I was surrounded by trees, and they all looked the same.

I turned to the left.

Followed the trail — until it ended. Then I left the path and zigzagged through the woods.

I hope I'm not late, I worried. What if Laura

leaves before I get there? I'll never find my way to the highway without her.

I ran faster, searching for the tree with the trunk split by lightning.

A buzzing sound made me stop. Bugs! A thick swarm of mosquitoes.

They buzzed around my head. Stung my cheeks. Yuck! Some of them flew into my mouth.

"Leave me alone!" I flailed my arms. Slapped my skin. Spit the buzzing bugs out of my mouth.

*Where is that tree?*

Still slapping at mosquitoes, I charged deeper into the forest — and heard the crackle of leaves.

Footsteps.

Animal footsteps.

I froze.

My heart started to pound.

Please, I prayed. Not a fox.

I waited for the animal to show itself.

A mournful howl rose through the forest.

I shivered.

Do foxes howl? I wondered.

I started off again. Tripped on a fallen tree limb. Hit the ground with a *THUD*.

"Ari, is that you?"

Laura!

"Yes!" I jumped to my feet.

Laura stepped out between two trees. "I was so scared." She grabbed her braid and tugged it nervously. "I thought you weren't coming. I thought you changed your mind."

"No way!" I said.

She took a deep breath. "They were so mean to me today."

"Who was mean to you?" I asked.

"The girls in my bunk. They're always playing mean tricks on me. They found out I was ticklish. So today they tickled me until I cried. I have to get away from here!"

"I'm coming with you," I said. "We'll escape together."

Laura let out a whoop of joy! "Thank you, Ari! All we have to do is cross the river."

Laura led the way. "The highway is nearby — on the other side of the river."

Laura led us deeper and deeper into the woods. She pushed low tree branches out of our way. We stepped carefully over rocks.

"Are you sure this is the way?" I asked. "None of this looks familiar."

A long, loud screech rang out.

Laura jumped back in fright.

We stopped. And heard another screech.

An animal shrieking in pain.

"We'd better not stand here," I said, trying to hide the fear in my voice. "Let's keep moving."

We walked quickly. I could hear Laura breathing hard.

"What's that?" Laura stopped.

The sound of laughter drifted through the trees. Hushed laughter. And whispers. Frightening, echoing whispers.

"Do you think there's somebody following us?" She bit her bottom lip.

"Uh — no. It's probably just the kids from camp. The wind must be carrying their voices."

"There is no wind blowing," she replied.

Suddenly the wind started to blow.

An icy wind from out of nowhere. So strong — it sent us staggering against a tree.

We wrapped our arms around the tree. The wind pinned us to the trunk. Whipped at us. Blinded us with its force.

The trees around us creaked and groaned.

"What's going on?" Laura shouted over the gale.

The wind blew harder.

"Why is this happening?" she cried in terror.

The wind stopped as quickly as it started.

An eerie quiet fell over the woods.

"I don't get it." Laura's voice trembled. "I've been in the woods every night. It's never been this creepy here before."

"How far is the river?" My voice shook too.

"Not far." She peered into a clump of trees. "I think it's right beyond these trees."

Laura started jogging. She disappeared into the woods.

"Hey! Wait up!"

"It's here!" she called. "Come on! I see it!"

I crashed through the trees. I found Laura standing at the bank of the narrow river.

"We just have to swim across and we'll be safe!" she said.

She grabbed my hand.

She tugged me toward the water.

I pulled back.

"It's very shallow. Don't worry," she said. "I've checked it out, Ari. We can wade most of the way."

"Are you sure? I'm not a great swimmer," I told her.

"I'm sure." She squeezed my hand. "Come on. We're almost home!"

Home.

That sounded great.

I followed her to the river's edge.

I took a step into the water.

"Stop!" a voice shouted.

I turned to the voice.

No one there.

"Don't move!" the voice ordered.

I raised my eyes — and gasped.

It was Noah.

Floating above us!

Floating just beneath the treetops.

Noah.

Ghostly pale. So light. Floating so lightly.

I could see right through him.

I could see the moonlight shining through his body.

"Don't move!" He floated down toward us. Hovered over our heads.

I shrank back.

"DON'T MOVE!" he howled. "I'M WARNING YOU — DON'T MOVE!"

et's go!" Laura grabbed my arm and pulled me toward the river. "Don't let him stop us!"

Noah swooped down.

"But — but — what *is* he?" I cried. "Is he a ghost?"

"This way!" Laura tugged me hard. "Hurry. Don't let him get you!"

Noah dove at us again.

Laura pulled me to the right.

Noah circled us wildly.

Trapped us.

"We can't let him catch us!" Laura yanked on my arm. "We have to get away."

We leaped for the river.

Laura crashed into the water first.

"Jump in, Ari!" Laura cried. "He can't catch you in the water!"

I took a deep breath. I started to jump.

Too late.

Noah grabbed my arm.

He yanked me away from the water.

Laura reached out and pulled me forward.

Pulled me toward the water.

Noah pulled harder. Pulled me back.

A sharp pain ripped through my shoulder.

"Stop! You're pulling me apart!" I screamed.

"Don't fight me!" Noah shrieked. "Don't you know who I am?" His ghostly voice rang through the forest.

"Yes! I know who you are!" I cried. "You're The Snatcher!"

# 25

Noah tightened his grip on my hand — and my fingers turned to ice.

All the warmth of my body seeped away. The chill of death swept through me.

"Let me go!" I screamed.

"Leave Ari alone!" Laura screamed at Noah. She grabbed my other arm with two hands. Tried to pull me free. Tugged me toward the river.

"You can't escape," Noah wailed. "Not that way."

He grabbed my hand tighter — and my arms and legs turned numb with cold.

I yanked my hand back with all my strength.

And finally broke free.

"I'm not going to be your next victim!" I cried.

"Don't talk to him. If you stop and talk, you're doomed!" Laura yelled.

Laura clutched my hand. She guided me into the river. "Come on! We still have a chance!"

"Listen to me!" Noah floated in front of me. "I'm not The Snatcher!"

"RUN!" Laura jerked me forward. "He's evil! Don't talk to him!"

"I'm not The Snatcher! I'm The Snatcher's *last victim*!" Noah cried. "SHE is The Snatcher!"

"That's crazy!" Laura insisted. "Don't listen!"

I dropped Laura's hand.

"I'm not The Snatcher. I'm a ghost," Noah said, hovering over me. "Half the campers at Full Moon are ghosts. We're all victims of The Snatcher."

"He's going to kill us!" Laura cried. "Please," she pleaded. "Let's go!"

"*Listen to me!*" Noah's voice boomed. "Each year, we choose someone to help us — someone to free our spirits. We want to rest. We don't want to haunt these woods."

Noah drifted up into the trees.

"There's only one way the ghosts of Camp Full Moon will ever find peace," he moaned. "Someone has to cross the river. Someone alive has to get to the other side."

My heart raced.

I glanced at Laura. Then Noah.

Who should I listen to?

Who should I trust?

Is Noah lying?

Is he The Snatcher?

"We ghosts chose you this year." Noah swooped down from the treetops. He gazed into my eyes with an icy stare. "We chose you to help us."

"He's a liar!" Laura's face twisted in fear. "He's trying to trap you here forever."

"She's the liar!" Noah howled.

Laura tugged on her long blond braid. "Please, listen to me. I'm trying to save your life!" she insisted.

My head pounded.

My body shook with terror.

If I could just think this through . . .

But it was no use.

I couldn't think clearly.

"Trust me," Laura begged. "I'll help you escape. You've got to believe me!"

I took a step toward the water.

"Don't go!" Noah wailed. "*She's* the liar! Did she tell you there's a girls' camp? There is none! She wants to trap you! She only wants to get you into the water!"

Noah whirled madly around us.

The leaves scattered in his path.

The tree branches trembled.

"You want to get me into the water too!" I screamed at him. "You *both* want me to cross the river!"

"But she won't let you get across *alive!*" Noah shrieked. "We need you to get across alive!"

My head started to spin.

What should I do?

Who should I trust?

*Who?*

I stared at Laura.

Is she telling the truth? I wondered.

I turned to Noah.

Or is he?

What should I do? I stood paralyzed.

"He's lying to you." Laura stepped up to me. Her lower lip trembled. "Please come with me. I don't want you to die. He's The Snatcher. You know I'm telling the truth."

"It's a trap!" Noah swirled around us. "She's evil. She'll say anything to get you into the river!"

I turned — and ran. I had to get away from them *both*!

I raced along the dark riverbank.

Crashed into tall weeds and shrubs.

Stumbled over rocks.

I glanced over my shoulder.

Laura charged after me.

Noah floated by her side in a race.

In a race — to get me!

My heart pounded against my ribs. I ran as fast I could.

"I can't wait anymore!" Laura cried out sharply.

She's crossing the river without me, I thought.

I stopped running. And whirled around.

"I can't wait anymore!" she cried out again. "Ari — you're the next ghost for Camp Full Moon!"

Laura leaped forward — and I gasped.

Her brown eyes glowed. They flickered in the dark — and brightened, brightened to red.

Her body flew through the air.

Transforming.

Changing — into a fox!

Changing into The Snatcher!

It lunged for me. Dug its claws into my shoulders. Snapped its teeth at my face.

The sharp teeth grazed the skin on my neck.

I grabbed the creature's front legs. Tried to pry them off me.

It dug its claws deeper into my skin.

I felt a sharp, burning pain. Then hot, wet blood as it trickled down my arm.

The creature let out a low snarl.

Bit my shoulder.

Lashed my cheek with its claws.

"Get off of me!" I yanked the fur on its back. I pulled frantically.

It brought back its head.

Opened its mouth wide.

It's ready to kill me, I realized. I have to do something!

Wait! The creature's ticklish, I remembered. That's it!

The creature's ticklish.

It said the other girls all tickled it.

I pried the creature's body away from my chest.

It let out low, menacing snarl.

I reached for its belly.

Held my breath — and started to tickle.

I dug my fingers deep into the creature's fur — and tickled.

A low growl escaped its throat.

Its head jerked forward. It snarled angrily. Pulled open its jaws.

This isn't working! Laura lied to me, I realized. What should I do now? *What?*

I grabbed the fox with two hands. Clutched it tightly. Tore it angrily away from me.

Then, with a desperate cry, I heaved the creature into the woods.

I heard a sick, painful grunt as it landed on the ground.

"Hurry!" Noah swooped down beside me. "You can save all the ghost kids at Camp Full Moon. Now's your chance! Cross the river!" he shouted.

I dove for the water.

"STOP!" Noah wailed.

I teetered at the river's edge — and stared in horror at the hands. Dozens of slimy green hands that poked up from the water.

Grasping hands.

Reaching up from the river bottom.

Grabbing for my legs.

Grasping for my ankles.

Horrible moans rose from the river as the hands stretched out for me.

I staggered back.

"The river is alive with monsters!" Noah said, floating beside me. "You can't get across by swimming. Those hands will pull you down. That's what The Snatcher wants."

I stared into the dark river.

The water churned and bubbled as more slimy hands broke the surface. Reaching toward the shore.

Grabbing blindly.

Ready to pull their next victim down.

"I can't help you! I can't save anyone!" I protested.

"Yes, you can. Look over there." Noah pointed to a low tree branch that crossed over the river.

"Climb along that branch! Quick! You can make it!"

I stared at the tree branch.

"I don't think I can do it," I murmured.

"Of course you can do it, Ari! You're a gymnast! That's why we chose you. It will be easy for you!"

"I'm not —" I started to say I wasn't Ari.

But I stopped. What's the point? I thought.

"I'm not sure," I said.

"If you cross the river, we'll all rest in peace." Noah's ghostly figure shimmered in the moonlight. "Please, Ari. You have to try. You have to defeat The Snatcher."

I ran over to the tree.

I jumped up.

Grabbed the branch with two hands. And pulled myself off the ground.

Hand over hand, I started to make my way along the branch.

Slowly swung over the forest floor. Moved further out. Out over the water now.

I gazed down at the murky river.

At the slimy green hands. Poking up. Sensing me. Grabbing at the air. Grabbing for my feet.

"I-I can't do it!" I screamed.

"You have to!" Noah wailed. "Keep going!"

I moved along the branch.

I kicked my legs, trying to kick away the grasping hands.

Low moans rose up from under the river.

My arms grew heavy. A sharp pain ripped through my shoulders.

"I'm not going to make it!" I groaned.

"You're halfway there!" Noah urged me on.

I swung one hand over the other.

Grabbed for the branch — and gasped.

"It's wet!" I cried. "The branch is slippery. I can't hold on!"

I dangled over the river.

Felt my fingers slipping.

The moans from underwater grew louder.

The hands moved with frenzy. Reaching up for me. Trying to tug me down.

"I can't hold on!" I shrieked.

My hands slipped off the branch.

I let out a scream — as I plunged toward the water.

# 28

I closed my eyes.

Falling . . . falling . . . floating.

Floating in the water.

No.

Floating in midair!

"I've got you!" Noah cried. "Don't panic!"

Yes!

Noah held me in the air.

We hovered over the water.

Below us, the wet green hands tried to snatch me from Noah's arms.

"Grab the branch!" he shouted.

I raised my arms. Grabbed hold of the tree branch — and heard a low snarl.

I gazed down — and stared into the eyes of the fox.

"It's back!" I cried.

"Hurry, Ari! You have to get to the other side!" Noah instructed.

I started moving across the branch again.

Hand over hand. Fingers aching with pain.

I saw the fox racing up the trunk. Moving steadily toward me.

Sweat poured from my forehead.

My heart hammered in my chest.

The moans from the river grew louder.

I struggled to hold myself up.

Struggled to keep moving.

"Hurry, Ari! You're almost there!" Noah cried.

I gazed across the river.

I *was* almost there.

Sweat poured into my eyes. Just a few more moves, I told myself.

The branch began to creak. Then bend.

It's going to snap, I realized with horror.

I swung one hand over the other. Tried to move faster.

Glanced to the side — and gasped. The fox leaped onto the branch.

I lost my concentration.

Let my fingers slip.

I tumbled from the limb.

The fox let out a low, menacing snarl. It jumped off the branch. Leaped after me.

I hurled myself forward.

Landed on the ground on the other side.

And heard a horrible screech — as the fox fell into the water.

The green hands rose up.

Grabbed greedily for it.

They fought for it. Pulled at it in a horrible tug-of-war.

The fox howled in pain — as the hands pulled it down . . . down . . . down below the surface.

And then, with a sharp *SNAP*, the branch crashed into the water.

I stood at the river's edge.

Gazed into the water.

Watched for the fox.

Waited for it to reappear. To struggle to the surface.

It didn't.

I stared as the hands eased their way back under the water.

My heart began to beat with a slow, steady rhythm.

I let out a low, long sigh.

Then shrieked in shock as a hand exploded from the water, grabbed my ankle, and pulled.

et me go!" I choked out.

With a desperate cry, I yanked my leg back.

Gazed down — and sighed.

Just a vine. Half floating in the water. Not a hand. A vine, half wrapped around my ankle.

My legs gave way.

I sank to my knees.

Struggled to catch my breath.

"Thank you," Noah called from the other side of the river. "You did it! You were so brave. Now we can all rest in peace."

Noah's ghostly form shimmered in the moonlight. Then he began to fade away.

"Thank you. Thank you." His voice grew fainter and fainter — and then he disappeared.

"I did it!" I realized. "I made it to the other side. I saved all the poor victims of The Snatcher!"

I leaped into the air.

"I really did it!" I shouted with joy. "I'm a new person! I really am a brave new person!"

I pumped a fist in the air.

"I *am* the man!" I shouted. "*I* saved the ghosts! *I* destroyed The Snatcher!"

I gazed out over the river.

The water was calm. It glistened under the light of the full moon.

Whoa!

Wait a minute!

I have a little problem here, I realized.

How do I get back across the river?

"Hey, guys!" I shouted. "Hey — anyone? Can anyone hear me?"

Silence.

"Hel-lo!" I called, cupping my hands around my mouth. "Hel-lo! Anybody! I need a little help here!"

Silence.

Crickets chirped. Trees creaked.

"Is anyone there?" I screamed. "Anyone? How do I get back now? *Anyone?!?*"

# About R.L. Stine

R.L. Stine is the most popular author in America. He is the creator of the *Goosebumps, Give Yourself Goosebumps, Fear Street,* and *Ghosts of Fear Street* series, among other popular books. He has written over 250 scary novels for kids. Bob lives in New York City with his wife, Jane, teenage son, Matt, and dog, Nadine.